Dear Seventeen

Nirjara Shinde

PAPER TOWNS
PUBLISHERS

First Published by
Paper Towns Publishers
72, Vishwanath Dham Colony,
Niwaru Road, Jhotwara,
Jaipur, 302012

Dear Seventeen

ISBN Print Book - 978-93-6185-583-2

Printed in India

To those of you who want to be everything at once
and nothing at all..

LOST

Dear seventeen, darling dreamer,
you found your home in paper pages.
You tiptoed in serene daylight
only to fill my world with dusky nights.
Dressed in smiles we both made a deal,
while the roses you bought me
had thorns intended to kill.
Tell me you came with swords and steels
because my body and soul are now
two different beings.

Dear seventeen, you cloud of dread and ink of red,
was it so easy to turn my heart inside out?
For you've etched those thoughts
on my skin now,
and I walk forever with a fear
that I might be read.

Dear seventeen,
you whispered to me the day you came,
and now I scream in silence
and laugh in pain.
It is time I bid you a farewell.
You've kept me on the edge all the year
and at times I've wanted to fall
so desperately out of fear.

Now is the time I jump
from this edge so high,
but rather than falling,
my heart wishes to fly.

I pick up the pen, with a myriad emotions
brawling to be claimed by this world
and begin to write.
As I write, I let my scars bleed
and bleed as wrenchingly as they were born,
I let my heart unfold and
unfold as vigorously
as it has been clutching those emotions all along.
I let my eyes flow and flow as cruelly
as they froze those tears,
I let my hands run,
and run as finely as they failed to stop
the voices in my ears.
And above all, I let my soul breathe,
urging it not to grieve and whine,
I let it breathe warmly, as warmly as it was
choked
by hands
none other than mine.

They called me
with voices of desperation.
And with each call that I answered,
I stabbed my scarred skin
only to paint their bloodless canvas
with the gush of my blood.
I burned my scorched flesh
only to illuminate their cold corpse;
drained all the warmth off me
only to drown them in the ocean of it.
Have I always had a fortune of love to offer?
I haven't.
Instead,
I gained it each time I gave it.
And all that love I weaved
from wrecked and ruined bits,
and injected upon the world,
has found its way back to me
through the essence of the cosmos.
It's highly compensating,
yet,
sometimes,
I laugh upon my own empathy.

I talk about love
dreamily, intently, as fiercely as thunder.
I talk about love with eyes full of wonder.
And it all seems pretty,
as long as it's only a dream,
for the thought of actually receiving love
makes my entity scream.
I'd ask, 'now what's this feeling called love?'
it's beautiful
yet tends to scare me away;
I'd admire it from afar,
but in its grasp,
a good price it makes me pay.
A price of discomfort.
A price of pain.
Is it my fault or is it the world's?
For what was supposed to be the cure
has always been a curse.
Tell me that the curse would one day be dead,
tell me I wouldn't be reminded
of a love
that exists only in my head.

The sun
saw its end
approaching leisurely
and bled splashes of grief,
while the sky
held the sun in its arms,
letting all its golden blood
spread
upon the evening,
And we call it a peaceful sunset.

Grief?
Back in the days,
it used to knock gently
on my door
with darkness, but enough light
for me to crawl back to life again.
Now,
now it is an everyday visitor,
a constant nightmare
draining all the light,
and the more I lock my doors for it,
the more it haunts me
in the dead of the night.

Love lurks in every corner of this house,
But the air of incomprehension
Has already found its place.
They know it, do they not?
The day I wanted to flake out in their embrace,
The floors saw me lying all tragic and helpless.
(*Tell me they saw me*)
The day I needed to wail in a lap,
I found myself crying with the bathroom tap.
(*Tell me they heard me)*
My hands are tied by their conceit,
I pour sympathy each time but fail to untie it.
Their words pierce through my flesh
Yet I never bleed,
I try so hard to destroy this cage
Until I no longer wish to be freed.

It was warm like sunlight
in my cloud of darkness,
they thought it'd burn me.

It was as cool as a breeze
on the fire burning my soul,
they thought it'd freeze me.

It built a wall of love and
protected me from the world,
they thought it'd imprison me.

It was breathing back life into me again,
but
they thought it'd kill me.

At times,
i wish, instead of tears,
my eyes cry out blood,
which would spill on the floor
and drown
me and my futile desire.

Was it your saintly love
that showed me my sanctuary,
or was it your detest
that grabbed me
to throw me again in this graveyard –
this graveyard that I had so longed to escape?
Did *love*
fix the broken pieces
or did *despise*
break them even more?
The ‘pieces’ are all I have –
they shatter and rebuild and shatter and rebuild,
and all I ask you, dear,
is to not question my fret,
for I look pretty only in the dark.
Because then, I know,
it’s not the absence of light,
but the shadows that make me seem worthy enough.

My gaze fell
upon the soft falling snow.
Peaceful, so breathtakingly peaceful.
Then I looked closer –
spots of black in the placid white
deceived my enthusiasm.
I looked closer and picked up a handful,
but the snow soaked my palm
shortly after,
leaving bits of wrappers and rags
that I had buried
not so long ago
crinkling in my hand.
I witnessed the lovely white snow poisoning
my eagerness
into disappointment.
And
my only fault was
I looked closer.

I’m scared of growing up.
Perhaps
things will take a turn,
tender
and slow,
or perhaps
I’ll have to face the challenges
I already know.

Perhaps
I will lose my track
in the dungeons
where
I’ve never been,
or perhaps
I will live a future
I have already seen.

Am I scared
of the shadows
of my thoughts
and all that has remained,
or am I scared
of facing a maturity
I have already gained?

So before I step
into those dreadful years
I'd want to foresee
what demons await me there,
can they be any worse
than the ones
who suck the air
out of my lungs, today?

Will they see me now,
now that I’ve painted myself red?
Will they hear me now,
now that I’ve swallowed all they said?
Will they feel me now,
now that I’ve snatched my soul apart?
Will they soothe me now,
now that I’ve poisoned the beats of that heart?
Will they find me now,
now that I’ve lost my old self?
Will they love me now,
now that I’ve hated myself?

And even if my heart
is close to erupting
and my throat throbs in anguish
in my agonizing sight,
I'd still be quiet.

Even if those words
gather in and around my throat
and strangle me,
and my soul shivers in fright,
I'd still be quiet.

So go on,
make your assumptions like everyone else did.
Because even if I'm sure I'm right,
I'd
still
be
quiet.

Sometimes I believe
that the voice built up from my throat
is fake,
for it contrasts the one inside me.
That the smiles and laughs I yield
are fake,
for they die out hastily.
That each drop of tear I shed
is fake
for it seems fabricated and synthetic.
The transparency of my flesh
is so sharply replaced
by opaques of insecurities
that now I can't see inside me anymore.
My body became a counterfeit and
dressed itself in shame-
shame of not knowing its own self.
And into the thin darkness,
I ask,
every night,
What
Am
I?

Here comes that one memory –
you try to erase it from your soul
or it would devour you whole.
It has to be gone, somehow.
You're forbidden to exhale it,
to let it loose,
so the other way you are bound to choose.
You let it disintegrate within,
to break your bones apart,
hoping it would be buried for eternity,
in some dark corner of your heart.
But little do you know, memories are brutal.
Oh, look-
You thought it lies in the grave of your heart
but it breaks free the chains,
spreading like poison all through your veins.
You try to strangle it to death
but it chokes you instead.
And now it's written all over your body
in a language of agony
that only the stricken ones can read.

Lord,
when you could have created me
a lifeless living person
with only flesh and a heart un-scarred,
then why did you give me
so much to say
that even speaking became hard?

Yes, I'm a pretty flower,
but one that didn't bloom well;
yes, I'm the serene moon,
but one on a new moon day.
Yes, I'm the bountiful ocean,
but one that vibrates and roars out loud;
yes I'm the glorious sunset,
but in a sky of stratus clouds.
Yes, I'm a star in the night sky,
one that's far enough to be seen by none;
yes I'm a harmonious poem,
but a poem that's poorly written.

I tell this haunting night
the tales of you,
and the stars fall for me a little more.
I am but a morose romantic,
yearning to gather our moments,
now dissolved into thin air.
yet all I do is speak to the void,
this endless black stretching before me,
hoping
it would take me back to you.

I stab this night with tales of you
and it bleeds your love upon me -
a crimson ache,
pooling where my heart used to be.

I like dark.
In the dark,
I can hide,
hiding is what I yearn the most for.
But this darkness
not only shields me from the world
but also traps my thoughts inside it,
not letting them
run away
from my mind.
My yearning to hide is stronger than these
reckless thoughts
and I,
I sit there amidst the darkness
as they slowly slaughter me to prove me wrong,
and they succeed,
they succeed every time.
So I hate, hate dark.
Yet again,
like a disobedient child,
I dive into darkness because I, I want to hide
and hiding is what I yearn the most for.

But can’t you see?
She is not living,
she is only surviving.
With each beat she is untangling
the sins of her past,
with each beat the untangled rope wraps her,
chains her aghast.
Can’t you see?
The shaky breath is a mere reflection
of the thunder roaring inside her,
the trembling legs, shaking hands,
are a mere reflection
of the volcano erupting inside her,
the racing heart is just a reflection
of the myriad thoughts racing in her mind.
She is stuck in a loop and there’s no way out-
can’t you see?
Her past still haunts her,
promising to haunt her forever,
and you may end her existence
extrinsically
but a fragment of her thoughts,
and of those haunting hunches
will always be left behind.
They don’t die with her.

I wonder why I wish to get lost
in this undying sorrow of loss,
but then I smile at a sky so boundless and blue
and breathe the air of what's left of you.

I wonder why I wish to walk down
the lanes of dead moments,
again and again,
but then those dead moments
bring me back to light
when all around me there's a draining night.

I wonder still,
with all my being,
among all this chaos
what made me keep going?
But then as sharp as lightning
the realization draws over me.
All my short and prolonged life,
have I not been looking for pieces long dead
and moments not even birthed, in me?

FOUND

But isn’t that you?
That flower in my garden
too pretty to be plucked,
that fallen leaf in the lake,
feebly stuck.
I’d look at the moon and ask too,
‘*Isn’t that you?*’
You,
draped in silver and spots,
elegant yet elusive,
you are everything I can never reach.
But then-
I bleed silver from my wrists cut wide.
I’d whisper again,
‘*Is that you?*’
or are you here,
immersed within me,
too absorbed to be true?

I don't regret
being the scrupulous and solemn,
un-cool and overthinking,
the quiet one amongst them.
For I know,
when the sun goes high,
they all need a shade,
and after every storm
the cosmos craves the quiet.
Because for every one of them,
I have something to offer from my heart
which is in
p i e c e s,
and for all of them
I have too many pieces to offer.
Too many voids to fill,
too many scars to heal.

"He's a boy – boys don't cry"
Here's what I say –
Latent as his heart might be,
it beats in a rhythm
just like you and me.
Yet why shall thou forbid his tears,
for even God Himself
grants him the privilege
to let out the bottled-up rage?
His eyes behold the same ache
that your soul acquires,
Yet up in the night sky he stares;
impeding tears desisted
by echoes of your senseless critics.
Burying that pain deep within
would only fuel his fire,
making him more fragile
and not the strong you desire.
So if you shall await
his long unseen joy,
let him drown in the solace
of "*you're just a boy*"

The wind touched my skin fiercely,
again,
and exhaled my agony.
The breeze caressed the trees
in a melodious way,
merrier than my burden of musings.
The thunder roared in grey,
again,
louder than my
frantically beating heart.
They hide me behind their enormous shroud and,
for a moment,
they take away with them
my weary spirit
and breathe back life into me,
alive and fresh,
once again.

Now,
I’ve dropped all my thorns,
for she seeks the fondle of flower
to forgive her sin;
I’ve tore open the curtains
to let the sunbeam caress her skin.
I’ve built her a safe place inside my heart
where she will uncover the agony through her art.
Do not you dare break her heart now,
for the thorns will make you bleed;
the sunbeam will burn you to ashes
and her art will pay your deed.
And this time, she won’t rise alone again,
thy shall be convinced.
I’ll rise with her,
rage-disguised,
for she
is a broken piece
of my soul
living in me long since.
She
is
me.

Scent of wood and earth,
skin of river.
Café and coffee,
one touch and a shiver.

Branches entwined,
fear freed into thin air.
Autumn leaf sings
a symphony of care.

Sunlight sneaking,
the clouds won't speak;
a dove's feather
brushing against her cheek.

Repentance in the soul
rushing again
into the past,
Aphrodite and her heart
together at last.

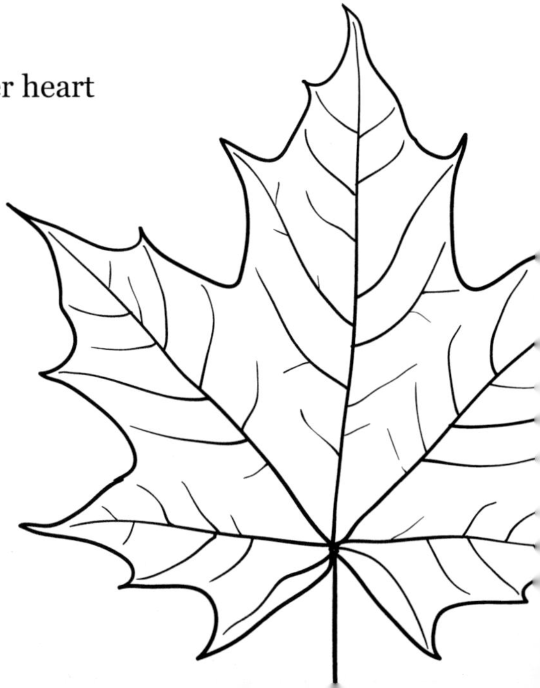

And it still amazes me
how gently
I'd pluck out a flower
from the tree,
whose branches
infused poison in my veins,
only to weave a garland
to adorn the tree with.

‘What is your dream?’
I birth a dream every morning.
I seek not to dream for a future,
for a future I’m not sure of.
I dream for today.
I wish, that today,
the sun shines through my window
a little more bright,
that the birds chirp louder
and fly a greater height.
That the rain, today,
falls on my skin,
that the mother in my neighborhood
strokes her baby’s chin.
I wish, that today,
my father smiles a little more,
my mother gets a peaceful sleep;
my brother cherishes his life,
and all of their smiles,
in my heart,
safely I keep.
So, I dream for little everyday moments,
for this is what life means.
I dream not for the destination,
but a journey full of dreams.

Oh Lord Zeus,
allow me to soar free
into that sky of yours
when I am nothing but a spirit
unleashed from bounds.

Lord Hermes,
speak my unsaid words,
that I kept safe in my heart,
to my friends and I shall seek solace in their
teary smiles that last a little longer.

Lord Poseidon,
let me drown deep
into the blue paradise
but only to feel wonders I missed while alive,
because *drowning*
is something not indifferent to me.

Oh goddess Aphrodite,
lift up the curse of love
that you've put on me
ever since I took my first breath
and pour purity among my people.

And Lord Hades,
long since you've waited for me.
Wrap me in delicate fantasies
and put into a peaceful sleep,
forever.

You told me
you see me all red
with eyes that speak the past.
The past that crawls upon me
with embedded spikes.
That I'm too tangled to sort out,
that my first approach is always a doubt.
You told me you see me all red,
yet when I look into those eyes of you,
why do I see a shining sky of blue?

What should I be ashamed of?
For letting this heart beat a little too much,
Or wanting to make it lifeless forever?
For staring into your eyes a little extra,
Or looking away to let you suffer?

For not speaking when they urged me to,
or exposing a lot when they urged me not to?

For letting you go
Or for letting you let *me* go?

ask me to grow flowers
and I will ask you to smile.
ask me to look at the moon
and I will look into your eyes.
ask me to pray
and I will kneel before your faith,
ask me to write a poem
and I will watch you take a breath.

you,
a warm ray of sunshine,
and i,
a cold cloud of thunder.
this fire burns brighter in the shadows.
we're caged in the prison of the world.

we try but do not break these cages,
God wrote us in the most forbidden pages.

but,
in another world,
I'll carve our book with blood as ink,
a world where fate is not a thing.
I'll build us a home
and paint us a sky,
where the stars will fall only for you,
you do not grieve, you do not die.
in that world,
you are immortal.
you will breathe forever in my poems.

tell me, dear rain,
for how long now
have you endured this pain?
it is not your season
yet here you come
tearing away the winds and dimming away the sun.

but you and me are alike.
so tell me, *for I know*,
have the clouds tortured you too?
to you they've been unfair
so you tore the silence with a cry of despair?

I've danced with you all these years
but this time,
you sound to me like a teenager
escaped from fret and fear.

they kept filling your heart time and again,
(I've been there too)
and now that your heart exploded,
and you burst in agony,
they blame it on you.

This kid wears joy on his face
as he chases those fireflies,
while
the light of a desperate echo for love burns in me.

He closes his eager eyes,
and makes a wish
as simply as he perceives that falling star,
while a burning rock plummets into my depths.
He closes his eyes,
and I never open mine.
He swims in the joy of
standing on that beach
as the waves hit him,
while I
remember drowning deep into the Styx.

He dances to the music of the clock
while
it pulls me closer to the inevitable end,
all the time.

tell this soul of mine to remain caged.

this soul lives far beyond the universe
yet somehow
it dwells in my skin,
where
buried flowers
lie in the graveyard
of this heart
that i carry within.

this soul,
this soul that dwells in me,
screams for the sky but buries my skin deep
into the ground.
this soul
longs to laugh
but strangles my throat and silences my sound.

tell this soul to not yearn for freedom,
tell this soul to remain caged.
tell this soul that each time it breaks the bars
they plunge themselves into my chest.

She wished yet did not wish
To be heard or seen,
And my eyes now reflect a silhouette
Of what could've been.

But what's special,
is that
no matter how black
my soul has been painted,
There always stays a light in me -
The light of life.
Forget the thorns,
I will always love the flower.
Forget the rain,
I'll always cherish the rainbow.
Because do you know what brings life
to my dead soul?
It is the petrichor after the rain,
All the beauty that dangles around me,
My mother's hidden praises for me,
My father's untold sufferings,
A child's face when I make it laugh,
And a starry night with my best-friend,
As quiet as we are.

I lived in a house with cracked walls and leaks,
Dust rooted on the windows,
and I couldn't fix.
I was locked from outside.
Moss grew on the walls and the
corners went stained,
The ceiling dripped gush of water as if it rained.

Earthquakes shook it, the noises were loud,
Loud, so loud, I never made a sound.

Shadows of illusion
used to spend every moment with me,
I was hiding my fear of them, they never let me free.

It was all a horror story by this time,
When a beloved knocked to remove all the grime;
And tossed me some key with charm in their eyes,
And said, '*dear, it is time to say your goodbyes.*
Have a long walk but thy shall return soon,
Till then this house will charm itself
to welcome you shining like moon.'

After ages of living in abyss I stepped out
in the felicity,
Stepped out through the door the
beloved had opened for me.
The joy and excitement caught a hold of me,
I locked the doors,
But lost the key.

As wretched as it was,
it was still my own heart,
after all,
it pumped blood in me.

I would choose to let go,
Each and every time,
And I'd paint golden any dark hue.
Yet every time you walk away,
I'm willing to walk to the grave with you.

Dear 17, my friendly woe,
You come to show what's true and fake,
Yet pain is all you give
And ease is all you take.
But dearest 17,
You carved me with melodies I'd always sing.
You are only a cliff I'm standing on,
While beneath you
the depths of seniority
await me.
It is time I jump now,
But a voice whispers –
It will go in vain, it is going in vain...

Dear 17,
You've pushed me so deep
And now I become a child again.

Cherish the people you know
you'd remember in your
last breath.